DID ADAM NAME THE VINEGARROON?

DID ADAM NAME THE VINEGARROON?

BY X. J. KENNEDY

ILLUSTRATED BY
HEIDI JOHANNA SELIG

DAVID R. GODINE · PUBLISHER · BOSTON

First published in 1982 by
David R. Godine, Publisher, Inc.
306 Dartmouth Street
Boston, Massachusetts 02116

Library of Congress Cataloging in Publication Data

Kennedy, X   J
    Did Adam name the vinegarroon?

    SUMMARY: Twenty-six alphabet rhymes about both
mythological and real beasts.
    1. Animals—Juvenile poetry. 2. Alphabet rhymes.
3. Children's poetry, American. [1. Animals—
Poetry. 2. Alphabet. 3. American poetry]
I. Selig, Heidi Johanna. II. Title.
PS3521.E563D5   811'.54   80-83964
ISBN 0-87923-357-5   AACR1

Printed in the United States of America

For you, if you will have it

NOTE

FOUR of these creatures are fabulous. Three are extinct. Two are constellations. The rest are actual. I have tried to favor things less commonly included in alphabetical bestiaries—although bee, crocodile, lion, snail, and others may seem pretty normal and ordinary.

Children may find the names of at least two creatures, Archeopteryx and Xiphosuran, hard to pronounce without rehearsal. I know I do. And so, at the beginnings of these poems, some help is offered.

I hope most of these pieces will strike both reader and listener as laughable, but not all of them are grimly supposed to be. I believe that, while a book of verse for children needs to be funny at times, it might as well, whenever it can, sneak in a little poetry.

XJK

DID ADAM NAME THE VINEGARROON?

ARCHEOPTERYX

(Say Ark-ee-OP-ter-icks)

A hundred forty million years
    Before it could be heard
By yours or mine or any ears
    This great-granddaddy bird

Stuck out its wings and gave a jump
    From marshes hot and squalid
And promptly splashed down on its rump
    Because its bones were solid

But kept on chirping till it burst.
    Now here we are to beg
One knotty question: which came first,
    Archeopteryx or egg?

BEE

You want to make some honey?
All right. Here's the recipe.
Pour the juice of a thousand flowers
Through the sweet tooth of a Bee.

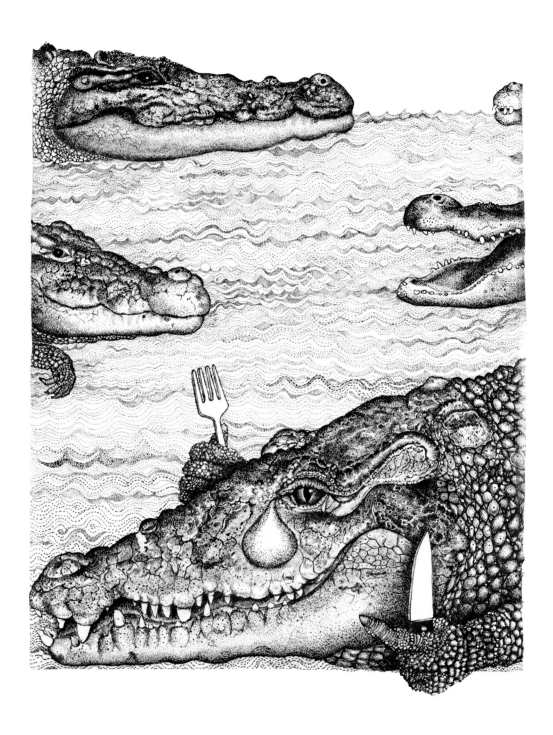

CROCODILE

The Crocodile's a social sort:
In bumpy green apparel
Crocs paddle round their jungle pool
Like pickles in a barrel.

The Crocodile can smile with style
And chuckle kindly, too.
Oh, they're the friendliest of beasts—
In fact, they're fond of *you!*

DINGO

The Dingo's not much of a dog
For keeping locked to leashes:
His kennel is a hollow log,
He doesn't dine from dishes,
He hunts wild juicy wallabies.
If you can bark his lingo,
He'll crack you jokes. But for a pet
I'd overlook the Dingo.

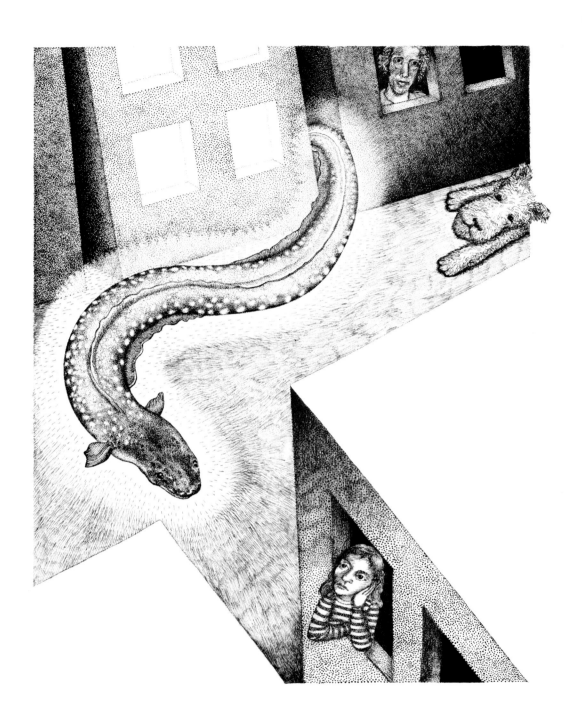

ELECTRIC EEL

Some think Electric Eel lacks looks,
Some others find it stunning.
A homegrown battery it packs
To keep its shocker running.

Why, you could light all New York's streets
And skyscrapers and stuff
With one Electric Eel alone
If it were long enough.

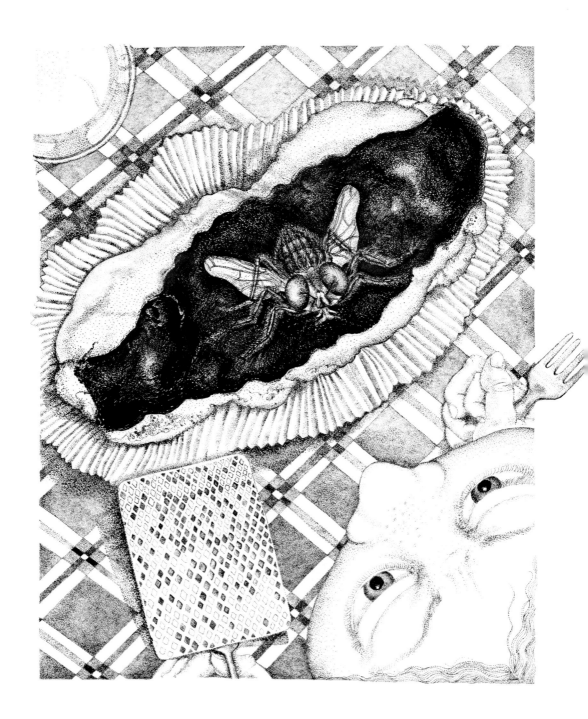

FLY

Flies seem to think the world is theirs.
　　Defiant of our swatters,
Along our chocolate éclairs
　　They strut, the cocky squatters.

How hard the Fly is to surprise!
　　It sees you through each shoulder
With twenty-twenty compound eyes
　　And gracefully grows older.

GOSHAWK

Golden Goshawk,
Slowly twist
Down from your sky.
Light on my wrist.

Let timid rabbits
Venture out—
See, I've for you
A rainbow trout.

Let skylarks soar
If skylarks would.
Come dream inside
Your leather hood.

HIPPOGRIFF

To look at this fictitious steed
You'd think some mixed-up farmer
Had crossed an eagle with a horse.
It carries knights in armor
Through cloudfields at terrific speed.
I wish the Hippogriff
Would take me for a ride. Of course
It's not real.
           But oh, if . . .!

IGUANA

Iguana demonstrates the signs
 Of somewhat hasty wrapping:
Beneath its chin a fold of skin
 Hangs downward, loosely flapping.

The quiet victim men forget
 In desert bomb-test sectors;
In Hollywood the pampered pet
 Of horror-film directors

Who need a live iguanadon—
 Oh, then Iguana's happy
To glue a few fake backfins on
 And play its great-grandpappy.

JERBOA

The tale is told that when the Ark
Was hoisting anchor Noah
Cried, 'Stop! what's happened to those mice
That jump?'
                His two Jerboa
Jumped for their lives, just made the boat,
And hit the deck *thud! thud!*—
Then Noah stroked his beard and smiled,
'All right now. Let it flood.'

KRAKEN

'Neath icelocked waves the Kraken lies
    In wait for passing ships,
To gobble them as you or I
    Might munch potato chips.

It's ten times huger than your school,
    More nasty than your teacher.
(Some Danish bishop full of ale
    Made up this baleful creature.)

One big fat soggy sponge below,
    Huge bulging eyes above.
It's nothing but a dream, you know,
    That you don't want to have—

Or is it? Take my Aunt Francine
    Who, swimming, was mistaken
By a nearsighted submarine
    For an emerging Kraken.

LION

Who bounded headfirst from the Ark?
　　Whose roar's a hurricane?
Who shakes whole jungles in the dark
　　With all his might and mane?

Lion. That's who adores to roar
　　And when you're with a Lion
The nearest house that has a door
　　Is good to keep an eye on.

MINOTAUR

King Minos had a Minotaur
    That all the people dreaded.
It gobbled fourteen kids a year.
    Incredibly bullheaded,

It dwelt inside a twisty maze
    That no one could escape
Till Theseus, shouting loud *Olés!*,
    Swung sword and swished red cape.

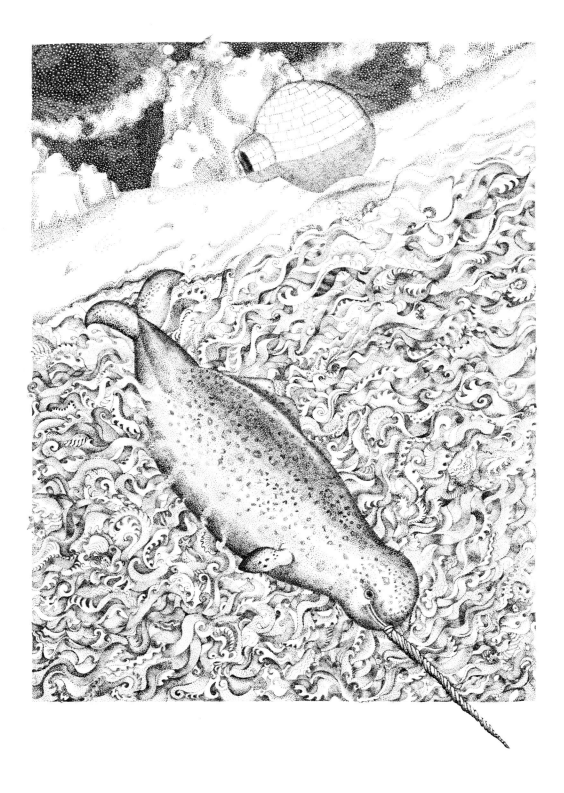

NARWHAL

Around their igloo fires with glee
  The Eskimo tell tales
Of Narwhal. Listen and you'll see
  This unicorn of whales

Through frosty waves off Greenland's coast
  Majestically advance
And like a knight come forth to joust
  Hold high its ivory lance.

OUNCE

The Ounce, a brand of spotted cat,
    Inhabits snow, not alleys.
Its summer hideout's high Tibet,
    In winter, it likes valleys.

Pale silver-gray, it makes its rounds,
    Beholds its prey and pounces,
And then an ibex (eighty pounds)
    Goes into sixteen Ounces.

PANGOLIN

Why in the world does a Pangolin
From the tip of its tail to the skin of its chin
On belly, back, sides
Wear plates like tin?
Why the stainless-steel stuff
For its coat and pants?

So a tiger can't break in
And let out its ants.

QUETZAL

The crested Quetzal seldom tours
Great Neck or Walla Walla.
It stays at home, official bird
Of sultry Guatemala.

Its head sports plumes of golden-green,
Its underparts are scarlet.
It trails a sweeping feathered train
As might some TV starlet.

Its taste in eats is delicate.
If you should meet a Quetzal,
The least polite remark to make
Is, 'Polly, want a pretzel?'

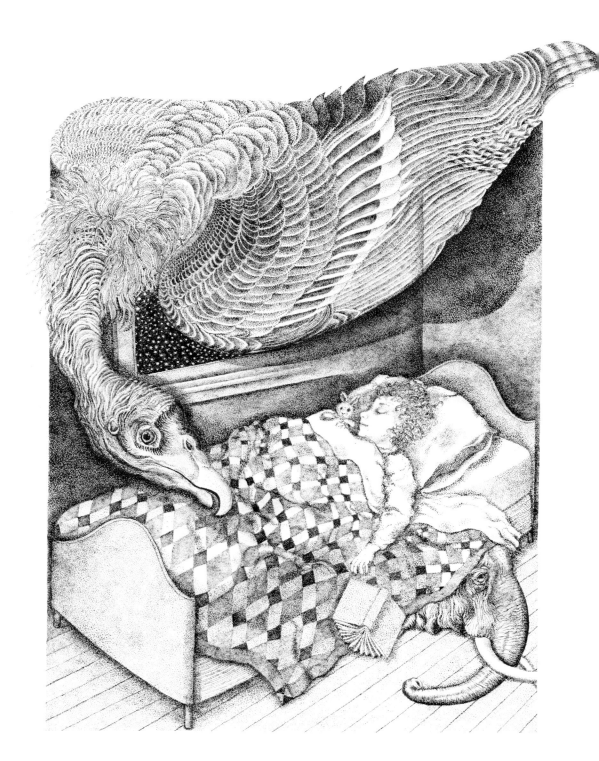

ROC

The Roc, when snacks are what it wants,
    Instead of flying solo
Will carry off whole elephants.
    Who says so? Marco Polo.

And in *A Thousand and One Nights*
    You'll read how this huge condor
Can spiral up to dizzying heights—
    Now *there's* a fact to ponder.

Why, just to circle one Roc's egg
    Took Sinbad fifty paces
And, turban wrapped around her leg,
    He hitchhiked to far places.

You've counted sheep? You still can't sleep?
    Try counting Rocs instead,
For then, if you should chance to dream,
    You'll have Rocs in your head.

SNAIL

The Snail is skilled at going slow,
    It spans the earth by inches.
Where it has been a trail will show.
    Its brave horn rarely flinches.

A dome of chalk upon its back,
    It lets a mayfly ride it,
And when it wants to take a nap,
    It curls itself inside it.

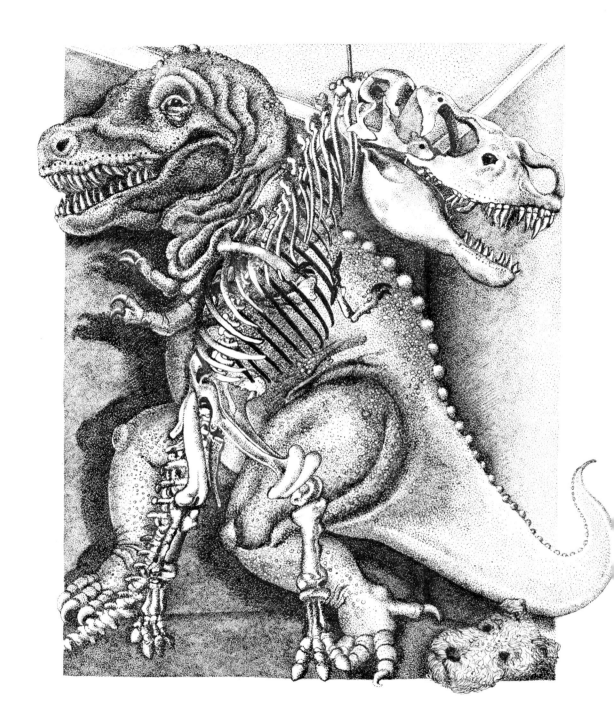

TYRANNOSAUR

A mean, late-model dinosaur,
  He walked Creation vastly.
His teeth were something to deplore;
  His table manners, ghastly.

With hungry jaws he laid harsh laws
  Upon the reptile nation:
By day and night his appetite
  Wiped out its population.

Yet tyrants, under Time's slow hand,
  Must one day bow their necks.
Now in museums—bones wired—stand
  Tyrannosaurus wrecks.

URSA MAJOR, URSA MINOR

The ancients, born before TV,
    At night skies had to stare
And, finding in the Milky Way
    Great Bear and Little Bear—

Vast furry bodies formed of stars—
    They added, to be funny,
Star-studded dippers, that those bears
    Might dip up heaps of honey.

VINEGARROON

The Vinegarroon, a scorpion
    With jaws like little sickles,
When filled with feelings of alarm
    Emits the smell of pickles.

What's that? A Vinegarroon? Keep still!
    Just tiptoe softly by it
Unless you crave a sour dill
    And you are on a diet.

WOOLLY MAMMOTH

When glassy glaciers glided south
And ice was all the rage,
This early-model elephant
Wore wool to suit its Age.

A hairy mountain ten feet tall
With peepers moist and misty,
It stood as solid as a wall,
Its twin tusks long and twisty.

By tribesmen in Siberia
A pack of these vast geezers
Was once discovered big as life
And fresh as fish in freezers.

XIPHOSURAN

(Say Zif-a-SOOR-an)

The Xiphosuran (if you like,
    The Horseshoe Crab) in all
Has little to it but a spike
    And legs on which to crawl.

The ocean beats it like a drum
    And, seen where low tide sloshes,
Four Xiphosurans look like some
    Old horse's spare galoshes—

Yet it has lasted ages. Won't
    You tell how, Xiphosuran?
Just hang on. Have one single point
    And backbone to endure in.

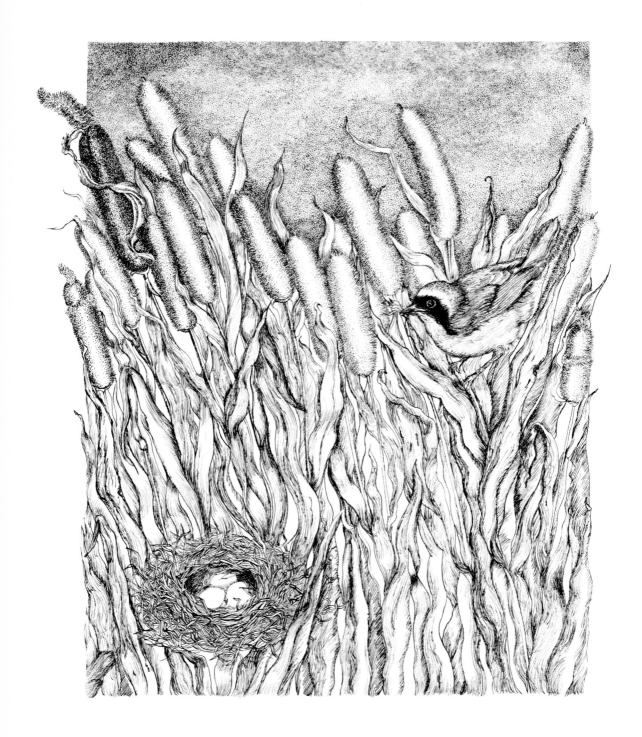

YELLOWTHROAT

Sway on that cat-tail, Yellowthroat,
    A moment till I ask:
Why does a bird who sounds so sweet—
'Witchery, *witchery*, WITCHERY, WHEAT—'
    Wear that black robber's mask?

Child, keep my secret from the rest
    And you shall have my thanks:
The grass with which I thatch my nest
(The long well-watered kind works best)
    I rob from river banks.

Zzzzzz

The Bee begins with letter B.
The reddest rose there is
Will wave him to her landing field.
His flight concludes with
                    ZZZZZZ.

DID ADAM NAME THE VINEGARROON?

was set in film Electra by G & S Typesetters, Inc.,
Austin, Texas. Designed by William Addison Dwiggins
for the Mergenthaler Linotype Company and first made
available in 1935, Electra is impossible to classify as
either 'modern' or 'old-style.' Not based on any
historical model or reflecting any particular period or
style, it is notable for its clean and elegant lines, its lack
of contrast between the thick and thin elements that
characterize most modern faces, and its freedom from all
idiosyncrasies that catch the eye and interfere with
reading.

DID ADAM NAME THE VINEGARROON? was designed
by Bob Lowe and printed on Glatfelter's Glatco Matte,
an acid-free sheet. Halliday Lithograph of West Hanover,
Massachusetts, was the printer and the binder.